This Walker book belongs to:

_____

_____

_____

Miss Hazeltine's Home For Shy and Fearful Cats

by Alicia Potter • illustrated by Birgitta Sif

WALKER BOOKS
AND SUBSIDIARIES
LONDON • BOSTON • SYDNEY • AUCKLAND

First published in Great Britain 2015 by Walker Books Ltd
87 Vauxhall Walk, London SE11 5HJ

This edition published 2016

2 4 6 8 10 9 7 5 3 1

Published by arrangement with Random House Children's Books, a division of Random House LLC,
a Penguin Random House Company, New York, U.S.A.

This book has been typeset in Perpetua Regular

Printed in China

British Library Cataloguing in Publication Data:
a catalogue record for this book is available from the British Library

ISBN 978-1-4063-6239-8

www.walker.co.uk

To my feral foster kittens,
who inspired this story,
and to Yodel, who stayed
~A.P.

To my purr-fect little girls,
Sóley and Salka
~B.S.

When Miss Hazeltine opened her Home for Shy and Fearful Cats, she didn't know if anyone would come.

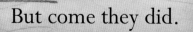

But come they did.

"He runs from mice!"

"She's scared of birds!"

"Can't pounce!"

"Won't purr!"

"Hopeless!"

"Worthless!"

"Afraid of EVERYTHING!"

Strays who could read Miss Hazeltine's
sign skittered in on their own.
Then there was Crumb, the most timid
of all. He dashed through the door …

and hid.

Miss Hazeltine began her lessons at once. In the morning, she taught Bird Basics.

In the afternoon, Climbing Up, followed by Climbing Down.

At night was Scary Noises.

Many cats received extra help
in Meeting New Friends.

Miss Hazeltine showed the
cats how to hold their tails
high. To arch their backs.
To think good thoughts.

Every day, they
practised pouncing.

The hardest lesson?
How Not to Fear the Broom.

Miss Hazeltine didn't mind if some cats only watched. She let them be.

Like Crumb.
Miss Hazeltine told him that, sometimes, she got scared. "I'm afraid of mushrooms and owls," she confided. "And I've never liked the dark."
She praised Crumb's love of pitch-black places.

Crumb lapped up every word. One day he
hoped to find the courage to thank her.
Still, he worried. Would he ever be brave?

Soon more cats came to Miss Hazeltine's home. And more. And more.

So many arrived that on a Monday at five o'clock, when everyone but Crumb was fast asleep, Miss Hazeltine ran out of milk.

"I'm off to fetch a bucketful," she told Crumb, "and will be back before dark."

Crumb watched her go.

But by the time Miss Hazeltine rounded
the road back home, the sun had set.

The heavy buckets
sloshed and slowed her

and her ankles were wibbly-
wobbly from all the pouncing.
Miss Hazeltine tripped …

and fell into a ditch.

With her ankle sore and
throbbing, Miss Hazeltine was
stuck. She shivered in the dark.
The pitch-black dark. Was that
an owl hooting? She peered
around. Mushrooms!
Miss Hazeltine tried to think
good thoughts.

Back home, the cats did the same.

But they were alone —
and very, very afraid.

They didn't know where
Miss Hazeltine had gone!

And they hadn't yet had the lesson on What to
Do When the Lady You Love Goes Missing.

But Crumb knew where
Miss Hazeltine had gone.

And maybe, just
maybe, what to do.

Crumb stepped
into the moonlight.

He arched his back.
He held his tail high.

He gathered the others.
Armed with nothing but the
old broom, the residents of Miss
Hazeltine's Home for Shy and
Fearful Cats streamed into the night.

Down in the ditch, Miss Hazeltine groaned.

"What will happen to the cats?" she whispered.
"And dear, dear Crumb?"

Yet something *was* happening. The cats felt it in their chests. With Crumb leading the way, they followed the sweet smell of milk down the road …

right to Miss Hazeltine!

At Crumb's *miaow*, the cats stared down the mushrooms.

They purred to
drown out the
owls' hoots.

And they pounced to be sure nothing lurked in the dark.

Then they formed a chain of cats to rescue
Miss Hazeltine from the ditch.
The broom made an excellent crutch.

Miss Hazeltine was escorted back to the
Home for Shy and Pretty Brave If You Ask
Us Cats (as the strays amended the sign).

"You're as bold as lions!" Miss Hazeltine told her rescuers. "And whether you stay for ever or head out into the world, I will never forget your courage."
The cats were so happy that they didn't even miss their milk.
Especially Crumb …

who had found a new favourite spot.

Alicia Potter holds an MFA in Writing for Children and Young Adults from the Vermont College of Fine Arts and is the author of the picture books *Fritz Danced the Fandango*, illustrated by Ethan Long, *Mrs. Harkness and the Panda*, illustrated by Melissa Sweet, and *Jubilee!*, illustrated by Matt Tavares. She is also a children's book reviewer for *FamilyFun* magazine. Alicia Potter lives in the USA, in Boston. Find her online at www.aliciapotterbooks.com.

Birgitta Sif was born in Iceland and lived in and around Scandinavia and America while growing up. She is the creator of the Kate Greenaway shortlisted picture book, *Oliver*, and *Frances Dean Who Loved To Dance and Dance*, both of which were endorsed by Amnesty International. Birgitta lives with her family in Cambridge. Find her online at www.birgittasif.com and on Twitter and Instagram as @birgittasif.

By the same illustrator:

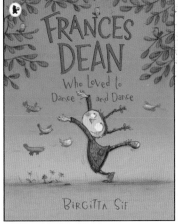

978-1-4063-4536-0

978-1-4063-6079-0

Available from all good booksellers

www.walker.co.uk